Rainy Day Duck

faith lessons from colorbox farm

TATE PUBLISHING & Enterprises

by Kaia L. Kloster
illustrated by Ruth Hanson

Published by Tate Publishing & Enterprises, LLC
127 E. Trade Center Terrace | Mustang, Oklahoma 73064 USA
1.888.361.9473 | www.tatepublishing.com

Tate Publishing is committed to excellence in the publishing industry. The company reflects the philosophy established by the founders, based on Psalm 68:11,
"The Lord gave the word and great was the company of those who published it."

Book design copyright © 2009 by Tate Publishing, LLC. All rights reserved.
Cover and Interior design by Elizabeth A. Mason
Illustrations by Ruth Hanson

Published in the United States of America

ISBN: 978-1-60799-835-8
1. Juvenile Fiction: Animals: Farm Animals
2. Juvenile Fiction: Religious: Christian: Animals
09.06.18

For my father, who would stand in the cold fall rain for me. . .
and would do anything for anyone who asked.

Introduction:

Welcome to Colorbox Farm!

The *Faith Lessons from Colorbox Farm* series is based on actual events that took place on our little hobby farm in southeastern South Dakota. Collecting one or more of at least a dozen different kinds of animals, some have asked me if I'm expecting a second flood! Our menagerie of animals has provided countless anecdotes that have entertained family and friends (and anyone I could get to listen!). I share them now with you. While animals may not communicate in so many words, their actions, postures, and expressions speak clearly if you take the time to listen. Just like people, they have personalities and preferences, temperaments and talents. Our critters have formed some semblance of community, and you may recognize traits in these animal characters usually deemed human qualities—love, empathy, faithfulness, guilt, mischief. It became clear that these cute animal stories could serve not only to entertain but to witness. While the beautiful sunset of the Colorbox Farm series symbolizes the majesty and splendor of our Creator, each story symbolizes a basic concept or message from the Holy Bible. As you read with your children, may the Holy Spirit touch you and guide you as you care for one of God's most precious gifts.

Fall rains. What a bummer. It didn't seem so long ago that we were enjoying the warm days of summer. Now fall was nearly over and winter was almost here. Not that there's anything wrong with fall or winter. There are great things about both seasons. . .

the beautiful fall colors. . .

sledding!

There was just something about those cold, blustery days between fall and winter—too cold to splash in puddles, yet not cold enough to turn the rain into snow. To be honest, it was just cold and wet and miserable!

I watched as my daughter, Taylor, pressed her forehead against the cold window. Letting out a big sigh, she turned and walked glumly back into the family room. I took her spot at the window and looked out over the dreary barnyard.

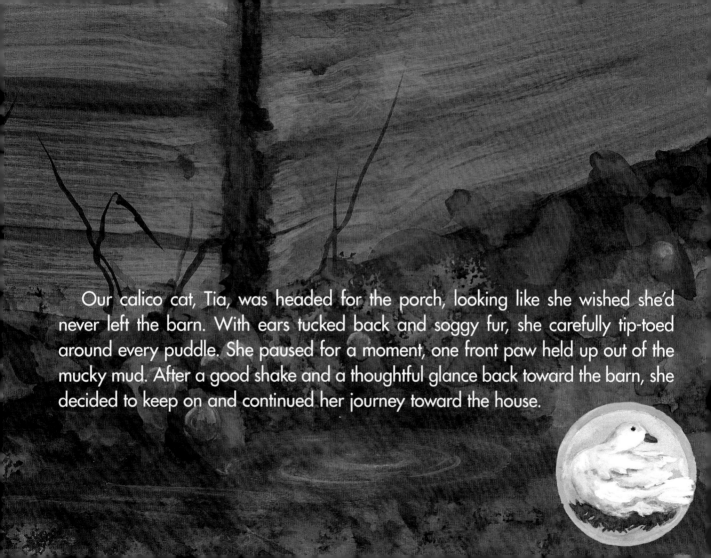

Our calico cat, Tia, was headed for the porch, looking like she wished she'd never left the barn. With ears tucked back and soggy fur, she carefully tip-toed around every puddle. She paused for a moment, one front paw held up out of the mucky mud. After a good shake and a thoughtful glance back toward the barn, she decided to keep on and continued her journey toward the house.

The big barn doors had not yet been shut for the winter. That naughty little Pygmy goat, Tildy, stood at the invisible fence that marked the difference between being wet and being dry. Surely there was some sort of mischief she should be getting into out there. But it just wasn't worth leaving the dry warmth of the barn.

In the pasture, the horses were all huddled together, tails to the wind. Their hind legs were hunched under them and their heads were down, muzzles nearly touching the ground. Poor old Red, he was shivering as if he'd been stuck in the deep freeze. They looked miserable. Sure it had rained harder than this, and the days would only be getting colder. It was the combination of cold air *and* being soaked to the skin. Everyone was hunkered down. Maybe the sun would be out tomorrow.

But what was that? Suddenly, there was a flurry of activity down by the barn. Why, it was Avery! The rainwater had collected into a large puddle. The little white duck was washing and wading, splashing and having a grand old time!

The cold rain was pouring down, but it only beaded up and ran off his oiled feathers. His fluffy down feathers were as dry as could be next to his skin. Avery would stretch his neck and spread his wings as if to welcome the downpour. Then he'd take a quick bob, scooping up some of the water and running it down his back.

One of his favorite things to do was to dabble in the muddy water. Snaking out his neck and sloshing the mud in and out of his bill, he would try to fish out any seeds or grain or bugs. I'm not sure how, but in the midst of all that muddy water, his feathers were sparkling white—but the tip of his bill always had a little ridge of mud.

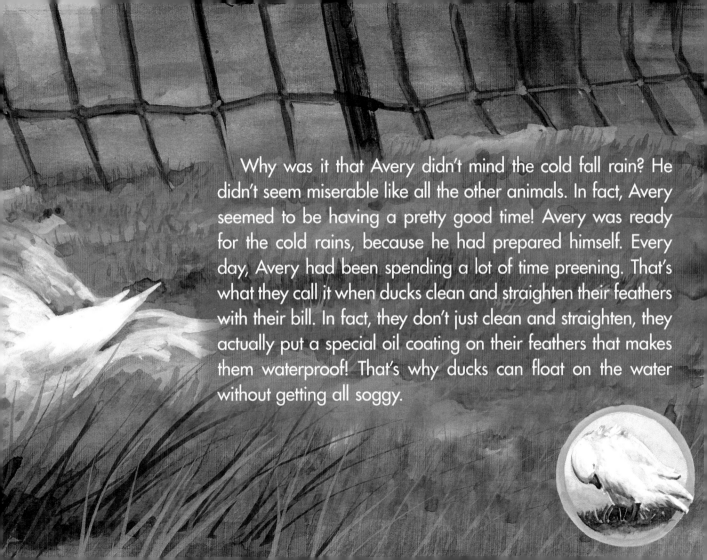

Why was it that Avery didn't mind the cold fall rain? He didn't seem miserable like all the other animals. In fact, Avery seemed to be having a pretty good time! Avery was ready for the cold rains, because he had prepared himself. Every day, Avery had been spending a lot of time preening. That's what they call it when ducks clean and straighten their feathers with their bill. In fact, they don't just clean and straighten, they actually put a special oil coating on their feathers that makes them waterproof! That's why ducks can float on the water without getting all soggy.

Well it seemed that his preening had been worth it. Rather than letting the cold fall rain spoil his day, he was making the most of it. While everyone else was worrying about getting wet and cold, Avery was having a ball!

And the peace of God, which transcends all understanding, will guard your hearts and your minds in Christ Jesus.

Philippians 4:7

Into the Holy Bible

Do you know anybody like the rainy day duck? Somebody who is happy, even during times when everyone else is sad or scared or worried? It's hard to understand how they can be happy when everything seems so miserable.

In Philippians we learn about the peace of God. Peace that passes all understanding. We can find the peace of God by taking the time to get to know Him better. Remember, Avery was ready for the rainy day because he took the time to be prepared. He spent part of every day preening, so he would be waterproof. If we spent part of every day reading our Bible or talking to God through prayer, maybe we would become "worryproof." With God's peace, we don't have to let everything that happens in this crazy world ruin our day. We can be at peace, knowing that God loves us and is always there for us.

So instead of running for cover, let's go out and splash in the puddles!

e|LIVE

---

listen|imagine|view|experience

AUDIO BOOK DOWNLOAD INCLUDED WITH THIS BOOK!

In your hands you hold a complete digital entertainment package. Besides purchasing the paper version of this book, this book includes a free download of the audio version of this book. Simply use the code listed below when visiting our website. Once downloaded to your computer, you can listen to the book through your computer's speakers, burn it to an audio CD or save the file to your portable music device (such as Apple's popular iPod) and listen on the go!

How to get your free audio book digital download:

1. Visit www.tatepublishing.com and click on the e|LIVE logo on the home page.
2. Enter the following coupon code:
   64cc-663d-7876-825a-af11-6715-d454-04dd
3. Download the audio book from your e|LIVE digital locker and begin enjoying your new digital entertainment package today!